CW00865507

MARS
Journeys to the Red Planet

Milly and Harry Pemberton

Title ID: 8711913
ISBN-13: 978-1722087517

Dedications and Acknowledgements

We dedicate this book to Mars, our brilliant school house group.

We would like to thank Sally and Ian Pemberton and Dr Neil for their help.

Contents

Bert on Mars

by Milly Pemberton

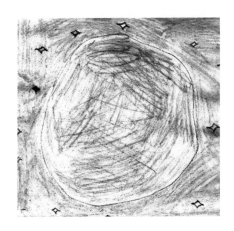

Once upon a time there was a man named Bert. Say hello Bert.

Now Bert had one wish, he wanted to go to the moon. So, he built himself a rocket.

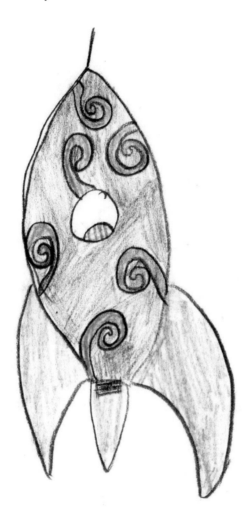

Whoosh and off he went!

But as he zoomed through the sky he missed the moon and went straight past it.......

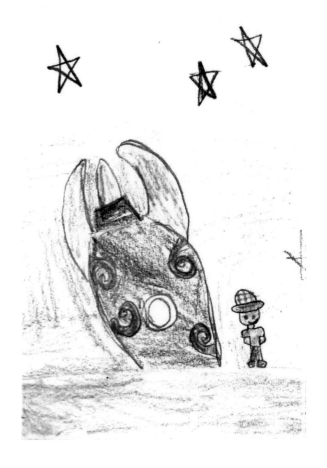

Crash! He landed on Mars!

His rocket nosedived into the ground and ice-cream from the engine (it was powered by ice-cream) splatted in Bert's face.

"Cold, but tasty!" thought Bert.

He wiped it off and got out to see what was there. A head popped out one of the craters, followed by the body of an alien.

"Hello, I'm an Malien. Malien means 'Mars-Alien'. My name is Dave. What's yours?" the alien asked.

"I am Bert" said Bert.

"Nice to meet you" said Dave. "Would you like me to show you around?"

"Yes, please" replied Bert.

Bert was shown all the passages and paths, halls and homes of the underground city.

They stopped at Dave's favourite snack bar to eat some lunch, which was yoghurt pizza.

So, after a while Bert decided it was time he headed home to earth but his rocket was broken after the crash.

"I know," Dave said, 'Why don't we make another?"

"Ok, but only if I can help you build it" said Bert.

They went to Dave's garage and after an hour of sawing and hammering, the rocket was complete, and its tank was full of spice-cream (which is space-ice cream).

With a good-bye hug from Dave, Bert got in his new rocket.

He blasted off back home, through the starry sky.

After an hour of flying Bert landed safely back
in his front garden.

"What fun I had" thought Bert.

"I wonder what I will do tomorrow……."

The Mars Quiz

Q. How big is Mars?

A. Half the size of Earth.

Q. How far from the sun is it?

A. 141633260 miles.

Q. How long is a year on Mars?

A. 687 days long (1.88 earth years).

Q. How long is a day?

A. 24 hours and 37 minutes.

Q. How many moons does Mars have?

A. 2

Q. What chemical makes it red?

A. Iron Oxide

Q. How much sea is there on Mars?

A. None. In fact, the land mass of Mars is roughly the same as earth.

Q. How big does the sun look from Mars?

A. About half the size it looks from Earth.

Q. Where did it get its name?

A. The Roman god of war.

Q. What shape is snow on Mars?

A. The snow that falls on Mars is the shape of little cubes.

Monty on Mars

by Harry Pemberton

One dark winter's morning Barry the self-taught space explorer was looking out his window at the few remaining stars and it was clear to him one of them was the planet Mars.

Barry had started to feel lonely. He sat in his comfy spinning chair that he had made from scrap metal and Monty the dog licked him. "I'll always have you" said Barry.

Barry sat there for quite a while and thought and he thought, and he thought. Until it struck him.

Right in the middle of his head! His model rocket had not got the correct type of string holding it up, so the weak string had just simply snapped. Although this did give him a great idea!

He immediately got to work. He was talented at DIY but very clumsy. There was paint and sawdust all over Barry's workshop.

Two weeks later he dragged his project out of the garage and there it was, beautifully shining in the morning sun.

It was a glorious space rocket. He spent the whole day filling his rocket with the special curry sauce that Barry discovered was super-efficient and he packed the rocket, including his many hats. It was dark when he finished, and he could barely get back to the house. Although it was easy to get back when the howling fire alarm went off.

He ran to the window and nearly got hit by the toast that had been flung out the window by his emergency evacuate toaster. It flew out the window past him and hit a surprised Monty.

After two hours of fire brigade checking and questioning about it they concluded that it was all a complete waste of time. Barry barely slept that night because of the drama last night but also, he was going to Mars tomorrow!

He was so excited when he woke up he nearly fell down the stairs. He barely had finished his breakfast, but he wasn't going to leave his toast. An astronaut needed is food! There wasn't anyone to help Barry take off, so he had to do it himself. 10,9,8,7,6,5,4,3,2,1, blast off!!!

Barry went whizzing through space avoiding meteors until he landed on Mars, but as he got closer something didn't feel right….

Barry got out his rocket and saw an alien. He wasn't worried because he knew they were harmless.

"It's horrible!" screamed the alien.

"What is?" asked Barry

"The Alens have taken over" said the alien.

"What are Alens?" asked Barry

"They are aliens with no eyes, but they have a great sense of smell" explained the alien.

He went back to the rocket to unpack, only to find that Monty had hidden himself the luggage hole. Monty looked so smug!

Monty jumped down and soon after Barry turned around to find that Monty was gone. Barry and the alien went looking in the aliens' land before finally going into Alens' land.

To Barry's surprise the Alens were evacuating.
One of them ran past screaming.

"He nibbled my toes!"

Alens take great pride in their feet.

They wondered round for a bit longer and
found Monty biting an Alen's feet.

They took Monty back to the rocket's kitchen and fed him loads of space bacon and Barry got some space bananas.

Then they all helped fill Barry's rocket with curry sauce and gave him a box of it to take home.

Barry went whizzing through space and landed perfectly back on earth.

He went back inside and tried some. It was lovely!

The End

We hope all our readers have enjoyed this book.

And we particularly hope that our teachers think it deserves some extra house points!

Watch out for our next books!

29258178R00021

Printed in Poland
by Amazon Fulfillment
Poland Sp. z o.o., Wrocław